The Rey

Rick Montel

The Eradication Archives

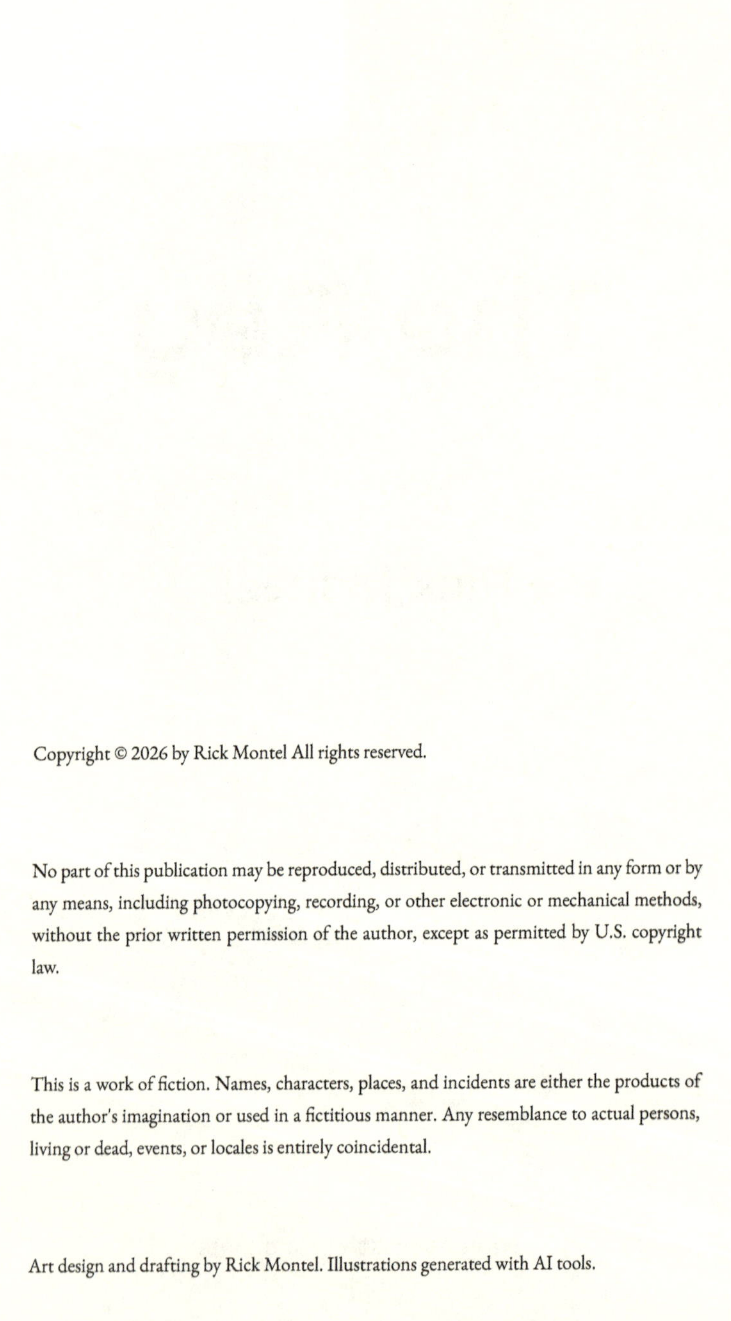

Author's Note

The Rey exists inside the world of **Echoes of War**, but it does not require it.

This novella was written as a standalone story—one voice, one life, one wound—set against the same fractured future that shapes the larger narrative. You do not need to know the Horsemen, the politics, or the full scope of the world to understand Rey. His story is meant to be felt on its own terms.

Within *Echoes of War*, history is often told through conflict, power, and consequence. *The Rey* steps sideways from that lens. It focuses on what remains after the walls are built and the decisions are made: the people who live with the aftermath, the quiet survivors who are not heroes, leaders, or symbols by choice.

Rey is not central to the larger saga because he changes the world. He matters because he refuses to disappear inside it.

This story is about grief without spectacle, resistance without violence, and the fragile act of listening when a controlled world would rather move on. If *Echoes of War* is about what humanity becomes under pressure, *The Rey* is about what it tries to hold onto when no one is watching.

You can read this book first.

You can read it last.

You can read it alone.

It stands where it needs to stand.

— Rick Montel

The Wall

PROLOGUE

The pounding came without warning.

Not a knock a neighbor or someone familiar would give. Not a request, but a violent, metallic hammering that rattled the front door hard enough to shake dust from the frame. Rey was standing in the kitchen when it started, a mug in his hand, the kettle screaming behind him as he tried to enjoy another quiet morning without his younger siblings. For a moment he thought it was a neighbor—someone drunk, someone confused. Then the pounding came again, louder, angrier, accompanied by a voice amplified through something mechanical and stripped of tone.

"Open the door. Mandatory evacuation." It demanded.

The power cut mid-sentence.

The kettle slowed until it stopped. Rey looked from the door to it, the lights blinked once, twice, then vanished. The house fell into an abrupt, unnatural quiet, causing the ringing in his ears to appear broken only by the pounding and the low murmur of voices outside—dozens of them, layered and restless, unintelligible.

Rey set the mug down slowly, morning officially ruined. His phone was already in his hand before he realized he'd reached for it. Glancing down he saw no signal. No bars. He toggled airplane mode off and on, like that had ever fixed anything. Nothing worked. Even the overhead lights, which he typically left dim all day were off.

The pounding didn't stop. Almost blatant rudeness and annoyance from the frequency of the knocking.

When Rey finally opened the door, dust and a gust of wind blew in and across the doorway with the street was already full of movement.

People stood in clusters, half-dressed, some barefoot, some crying, some shouting questions no one answered. Armed figures moved through them in pairs, faces hidden behind dark visors, weapons held low but ready, not for the people... for something else. Vehicles idled at odd angles, doors left open. Somewhere down the block, a child screamed until a parent hushed them too quickly.

"Grab essentials only," one of the figures said, voice flat. "You will not be returning." Another said from a different part of the crowd. A set of statements seemingly repeated fairly frequently.

"What?" Rey said to the one deputy standing near his porch, the word coming out useless and thin.

The figure didn't look at him. "Now." He said, more to the crowd but Rey felt it directed towards him as well.

Rey went back inside on instinct, not thought. The house felt smaller without the lights, the familiar rooms suddenly foreign as though his world perspective is shifting. His eyes landed on the guitar leaning against the wall near the couch, strings dull with age, a soft case scuffed and patched with old patches sewn on. He grabbed it, slung the strap over his shoulder, then stopped, unsure what else mattered.

Clothes. Shoes. A jacket. Things which he had typically also at the ready in a go-bag for his night gigs. He put the jacket on and clipped the rest onto the strap of his guitar bag which held onto him crossbody.

On his way out he hesitated in the hallway, staring at the closed doors to his siblings' rooms. Lidia's posters still clung to the walls, edges curling. Mateo's textbooks sat stacked on the floor where he'd left them last semester. Rey stood there too long, like if he stayed still enough the moment might pass and the morning would revert to routine. That he'll get the call from his little brother saying he and his little sister were okay.

It didn't and the call never came.

The deputy took a half step back towards the doorway which was still open. "Sir, we got to get you moving."

Rey rounded the corner and now outside, the crowd was still steadily moving.

"What's going on?" He asked the deputy. No response but the eyes that he was met with was almost as unsure as he was. Just someone doing a job, hoping it is for the best.

"Let's go, sir, lock up" He said calmy. Rey nodded and locked the door, walking with the deputy down towards the crowd. They were being herded toward the main road, toward the distant shape that had loomed on the horizon for years without explanation—the Wall. It rose far beyond the town limits, a jagged line of steel and concrete cutting the sky in half. Construction had started long before anyone knew why. People joked about it at first. Borders. Storm control. Government waste.

No one was laughing now. No time too.

Rey moved with the crowd, pulled along by momentum more than choice but it felt wrong. The air buzzed with overlapping voices, fragments of panic bouncing from person to person like static. Someone shouted about a quarantine. Someone else said it was a drill. A woman sobbed into her phone even though it hadn't worked in minutes, or is it working now? Rey checked his again. Nothing.

A hand grabbed his sleeve.

"Rey."

He turned and saw Amara forcing her way through the bodies, hair pulled back, face flushed and sharp with fear. Relief hit him harder than it should have, someone familiar.

"Thank God," she said, breathless. "I couldn't find you or reach you."

"Do you know what's happening?" he asked.

She shook her head. "No. I tried calling—nothing works." Her eyes shifted to the Wall and back. "Not sure even the cops know..."

They fell into step together as the road narrowed, concrete barriers funneling the crowd toward a single direction. The Wall grew taller with every step; its surface scarred with seams and scaffolding marks like it had been rushed into existence, Rey hasn't been into the city lately so this is the closest he's ever gotten to the Wall. Above them, drones hummed into position, dark shapes against the washed-out sky.

As the crowd seemed to settle away from a chaotic behavior and more as stable cattle accepting fate, Amara leaned closer. "I talked to your sister last night."

Rey looked at her. "Lidia?" She nods.

"She said something about coming home early. Some quarantine rumor in Colorado. They were going to surprise you."

The words landed wrong. Too late. Too sharp. Rey could've had them in his arms right this moment, if he only had known.

"Mateo's with her," Amara added quickly. "They're together." Trying to calm the buildup she sees brewing.

Rey nodded, but the sound around him dimmed, the crowd fading into a dull roar. He pictured them on a campus somewhere sunny and untouched, laughing about how dramatic everyone back home always was. He pictured his phone lighting up with her name.

Again, it didn't.

The line slowed as they reached the outer perimeter. Armed personnel formed a corridor, bodies rigid now, posture no longer casual, these guys definitely know more. Scanning towers flanked the entrance, lights sweeping over faces, pausing, moving on. The air smelled like ozone, dust and fresh mechanical construction.

Beyond the opening in the Wall, the skyline rose in sharp relief—Vegas, intact and glowing, glass towers catching the midday sun like nothing was wrong. Like the world hadn't just tilted. Near the opening on the interior of the wall looked to be a FEMA encampment.

A murmur rippled through the crowd as people saw it.

They moved through in groups. Step forward. Pause. A burst of light. A tone. Then waved on. Scanners did the scanning for something no one knows what.

Rey's chest tightened the closer they got. His breath shortened, each inhale shallow and unsatisfying. He tried to slow it but failed, causing a chain reaction of faster breathing.

Amara's fingers brushed his wrist, grounding him. "Hey. Stay with me."

A siren wailed somewhere behind them.

Then another, as a chorus.

The tone shifted—sharper, urgent. The drones overhead repositioned quickly, their hum deepening. The armed figures straightened, weapons coming up not quite aimed but no longer neutral, active ready.

"What's happening?" someone shouted from the back of the line.

The Wall shuddered.

A low mechanical groan rolled through the ground, felt more than heard as though a tremor. Rey turned instinctively, and what he saw behind them tore something loose in his chest. The crowd had changed and no longer stable.

Panic spread faster than sound. People pushed, surged forward, abandoning the careful order they'd been forced into. Someone fell. Others stumbled over them. Shouts turned into screams as the realization hit all at once. Chaos in full swing.

The doors were moving.

Massive slabs of reinforced steel began sliding inward, slow at first, then faster, the gap narrowing with an inevitability that stole the air from Rey's lungs. The drones screamed now, alarms flaring red across the sky, they opened fire at the rear of the crowd.

"Move!" one of the armed people yelled.

The line collapsed in a disorganized mess.

Bodies slammed together, momentum carrying them forward whether they wanted it or not. Rey felt himself lifted, feet barely touching the ground as the press of people forced him toward the opening. He lost sight of Amara for a heartbeat, then found her again, her face pale, eyes wide. He reached out and grabbed hold.

The sound—he would remember the sound more than anything.

Metal grinding. Flesh hitting steel. A wet, indistinct impact that sent a red mist spraying upward, catching the light before drifting down over screaming faces.

The doors didn't stop. The metal cogs grinding, relentlessly.

People were crushed against them, screams cut short as the gap narrowed. Hands reached out, fingers clawing at nothing. Someone's shoe came off and vanished beneath the crowd.

Rey was shoved forward, stumbling through the threshold as the doors sealed behind him with a final, echoing slam. Final gasps of air from lungs instantly stopped.

Silence followed—not true silence, but something close. The screams were gone. The drones settled into a steady hover now with the doors sealed. The survivors stood frozen just inside the Wall, staring back at what wasn't there anymore.

Rey turned slowly.

The Wall stood whole and unbroken, clean as if it had never opened at all. Only red stains revealing the crease of what would be the center of the door.

He dropped to his knees without realizing it, the guitar knocking against the concrete. His hands shook, useless at his sides. Somewhere nearby, someone retched. Someone else laughed—a thin, broken sound that didn't belong to joy.

Rey looked at the skyline ahead of him, bright and indifferent.

Then he looked back at the Wall.

And understood, with a clarity that burned, that nothing he had been before mattered anymore.

BEFORE THE SILENCE

1

The morning had been too quiet.

Rey noticed it even before the pounding, even before the lights died and the world turned foreign. The kind of quiet that didn't feel earned. As if the house was holding its breath. Like the walls were listening for something.

He had spent years hearing footsteps in this place—Lidia's heavy ones when she was mad, Mateo's lighter ones when he was trying to sneak past without being noticed. Cabinets opening and closing. Music from a phone speaker drifting under a bedroom door, Lidia of course. The argument about whose turn it was to take out trash which was typically playful. The laughter when Mateo tried to cook and set off the smoke alarm and swore it was "part of the process." Normal noise. Annoying noise. Noise you didn't notice until it was gone.

Which now it was.

Lidia and Mateo had been on the road for barely two days. Two days into a trip that was supposed to be a week, maybe less if Mateo got tired of California traffic and called it early, deciding to go to college nearby instead, hopefully. Rey had watched them pull away with the kind of face he tried not to show them—proud and tense at the same time, like if he smiled too hard it would turn into worry.

"Text me when you land," he'd told them, like service was always a guarantee. Like the world couldn't just decide it was done. There was no way.

Mateo had rolled his eyes, already halfway into the driver seat. "Rey, we're going to California."

Rey dumped his hands into his pocket and a little tilt of the head. "Exactly." Mateo chuckled.

Lidia had leaned out of the passenger window, hair in her face, and made a heart shape with her hands because she thought it was funny watching him pretend, he didn't care. "We'll be fine. Go write your rock songs! We'll bring you back real tacos." She flashed the bull sign with her fingers. He chuckled, returning it to her.

He walked around the car making sure to tell them to lock the doors. To keep their phones charged. To call if anything felt off. The worried image he tried to hide was poking out.

He didn't tell them what he really meant.

Don't disappear. Hurry back.

The trust, it handled the bills. The mortgage was paid. The utilities ran on autopay. Money wasn't the problem. It never had been, not the way people assumed. Rey could've quit his day hustle years ago if he wanted to in order to spend more time at home raising them. Could've moved closer to the city. Could've bought better gear rather than use Jax's hand-me-down guitar. Could've done the whole thing like other musicians did—chasing the next gig like it was oxygen.

But money was never what kept his life together, Luckly.

It was responsibility, the routine. It was waking up early because Lidia had school and needed someone to pretend they didn't hear her crying in the bathroom after she'd fought with a friend because something related to graduation that was coming up. It was picking Mateo up from practice because he forgot his ride again. It was sitting at the kitchen table with a stack of mail and a pen, reading bills like they were threats, even though he knew it was never an issue.

It was being the adult in the house even when he didn't feel like one.

That was what he was when he woke up that morning. The adult. The guardian. The one who stayed.

It was only later that he would understand the quiet had been a warning.

Rey stood at the sink and let the hot water run, not because he needed it, but because the sound filled the room. The kettle whistled behind him and he didn't rush. No one was yelling from a bedroom. No one was asking him to find a missing charger or explain why the Wi-Fi was slow. No one was stomping down the hallway to say they needed a ride in ten minutes. He wanted to not be his sibling's father for a moment.

He'd wanted this—this small freedom, this empty space.

Now he was standing in it, and it felt wrong.

The mug in his hand had an old chip on the rim. He'd meant to replace it months ago, but he liked that it was the same mug their mom used to drink coffee from before she got sick. Not because he was sentimental, not because he sat around missing the past like a movie.

He just didn't like changing things that already survived.

Rey glanced over almost instinctually to a desire to find cover which landed his eyes on his guitar which was across the room, leaning where he always kept it. Not a trophy. Not decoration. Just there, like a tool waiting to be picked up, where he can still hear Jax's voice during one of their band practices back in the day. The case, flopped on a stand next to it was soft and worn, patches sewn on from old gigs and old places, things that used to matter when the world was smaller. Rey had the go-bag half packed already because that was how his life worked now. If someone called him last minute for a bar set, he didn't have to scramble. He could grab and go. No stress. No excuses. A solo act since his friends moved on to do things in their own lives outside of music.

He'd been trying to do it right lately. Not fame-right. Not social media-right. Just... real, authentic.

He was tired of playing the same covers in the same dives for the same people who only half listened until the chorus of something familiar hit and they shouted the lyrics back like it was their own story. He didn't blame them for it. People needed something to hold onto. In a place like this, the bars weren't just bars. They were confessionals. Safe rooms. Places people could pretend the world was still simple for a couple hours.

Rey had been doing it long enough to know the difference between a crowd that wanted noise and a crowd that wanted to feel something.

The second kind was rare, of course as more often than not people just wanted the drinks. That was their confessional.

Those were the nights he lived for. The nights he played one of his own songs and the room didn't talk over it. The nights he saw someone stop mid-drink and stare at the stage like the words had pulled something out of them they didn't want anyone to see. The nights an old man would walk up after and say, "I don't even like music... but I liked that."

Those were the nights that made him think maybe he wasn't wasting time.

He taught kids guitar lessons on weekdays. Not because he needed the money—because he liked it. Because kids were honest in a way adults weren't. They didn't pretend. If you sounded bad, they told you. If they were bored, they showed it. If they learned a riff and their eyes lit up, it felt like watching fire catch.

Some of their parents treated him like a babysitter. Some treated him like a therapist. Some treated him like a miracle because their kid finally wanted to focus on something that wasn't a screen.

Rey didn't take it personal. Everyone was tired. Everyone was trying.

There was a boy named Eli who came every Wednesday, small for his age, always wearing a hoodie even in summer. He never spoke above a mumble. The first lesson he barely touched the guitar like it might bite him. By the fourth lesson he was playing simple chords and looking at Rey like he was waiting for permission to exist.

"Stop apologizing," Rey had told him.

Eli blinked. "I'm not—"

"Yes you are," Rey said, not harsh, just real. "You keep saying sorry like you're taking up space. You're allowed to be here."

The kid didn't answer. He just nodded and played the chord again, a little cleaner.

Rey liked moments like that. Quiet ones. Small wins no one clapped for.

Because that was life now. Not big moments. Not celebrations. Just surviving and stacking tiny wins until something looked like a future.

He had been thinking about a new song for weeks. Not a heartbreak song. Not a "sad boy with a guitar" song people expected from him. Something different. Something about the Wall.

He didn't say it out loud often. People in town did. The Wall was like weather now. It existed. It loomed. It was always in the distance, a gray spine against the horizon. They built it slow, section by section, like it was normal to fence the world in. Like it was normal to have drones occasionally pass overhead and pretend you didn't see them.

Rey had driven close once, years ago. Just to look. Just to feel the scale of it. The closer he got, the more the air felt heavy, like the whole thing pulled on him. He remembered thinking it didn't look like protection. It looked like a verdict.

He backed up and drove home without telling anyone why.

His phone buzzed on the counter that morning. He glanced at it out of habit, expecting maybe a meme from Mateo or a blurry selfie from Lidia making fun of California.

It was Amara.

Mara: you alive?

Rey snorted once, barely a laugh. His thumbs hovered.

Rey: unfortunately

The reply came quick.

Mara: dramatic. u working today?

He looked around the empty kitchen. The quiet stared back.

Rey: guitar lessons later. thinking about writing

Mara: writing or staring at your wall again

He exhaled through his nose. She wasn't wrong. She knew him too well, in a way that didn't require romance to explain it.

Rey: both

A pause. Then:

Mara: come by the dive tonight. i'll bring the usual crew. you need to be seen

He stared at the message longer than necessary, like the words had weight.

You need to be seen.

People said things like that when they thought someone was fading.

He typed:

Rey: i'll see

A minute later:

Mara: that means yes. don't make me drag you

Rey set the phone down and glanced at the guitar again. It leaned where it always leaned, quiet, patient. Like it didn't care if he played or not.

He did care though.

He had this image in his head lately—Lidia walking into one of his gigs, surprise on her face because she'd never really watched him play for real. Not the way he played when the room mattered. Mateo beside her, pretending he wasn't proud. Both of them hearing a song and realizing their brother was something beyond a guardian and a guy who cooked meals and paid bills.

He wanted that.

Not because he needed praise.

Because he wanted them to see him as a person too.

Rey lifted the mug to his mouth and took a sip. The coffee was too hot and bitter. He made a face. In the old days, someone would've laughed at him for it. Lidia would've said, "You're such a baby," and Mateo would've copied the face just to make her laugh.

Now there was only the kettle screaming.

Rey turned toward it and that was when the pounding came.

Not a knock a neighbor or someone familiar would give. Not a request, but a violent, metallic hammering that rattled the front door hard enough to shake dust from the frame.

And in that exact moment, with his hand reaching toward the stove and his mind still stuck on a text message and the idea of a bar gig later that night, Rey's world cracked open.

The kettle screamed.

Then the power died.

And the quiet that followed was so complete it felt like the house itself had been unplugged from reality.

AMARA

2

R ey didn't remember the first time he met Amara.

Not because it wasn't important, but because it had been normal. Before everything turned into markers and before-and-after lines. They'd been in the same halls, same classes, same town where everybody knew everybody, and memories blurred together when you stayed in one place long enough. It wasn't like some movie moment where he looked up and saw her glowing in a doorway and knew his life had changed.

He just knew she was there. Always.

Amara Torres. Mara, because she hated how people tried too hard to say her full name like it was something delicate. Mara because it sounded like a warning and a laugh at the same time. She was the kind of girl who could walk into a room and immediately locate the weak point in it. Not to hurt anyone. Just... to understand the shape of the space.

Rey had always liked that about her.

She didn't float through life. She moved through it like she was paying attention.

That night, before the world broke, she found him at the dive like she always did.

Not the nice bar. Not the place with the polished wood and the fake neon signs pretending the town had a nightlife. The real one. The place that smelled like old beer soaked into the floorboards and fried food that never fully left the air. The place with the same cracked pool table, the same stools, the same bartender who had stopped asking people what they wanted years ago.

Rey's guitar was on his back when he stepped inside, case slung crossbody like a habit. He wasn't playing yet. He was just there. Showing face like Mara said. Letting people know he still existed.

The room was loud in the way small-town bars got loud—familiar voices, familiar laughter, stories repeated for the tenth time like tradition. A few heads turned when he walked in. Not because he was famous. Just because he was part of the furniture. Part of the routine.

He saw Mara's group in the corner booth. She wasn't sitting. She was half-standing, leaning on the table with one knee up on the seat, talking with her hands, eyes bright. She wore a black hoodie under a denim jacket, hair pulled back, hoops in her ears catching the low light. She looked like she belonged anywhere. Like she'd survive anywhere.

When she noticed him, she pointed like she'd caught him doing something illegal.

"There he is," she said loud enough for the booth to hear. "Look who decided to leave his cave."

Rey didn't smile right away. He never did. He let it build slow, like a defense.

"Don't start," he said, sliding into the edge of the booth.

Mara's eyes flicked to his guitar case. "I'm always gonna start. You know that."

Her friends shifted to make space. People Rey knew by name and not much else. Good people. Loud people. The kind who didn't ask deep questions unless they were drunk enough to regret it later.

They all liked Mara. That was the thing about her. She was sharp, but she wasn't mean. She had the kind of energy that made people feel included even while she was roasting them.

"Rey!" one of them said, raising a glass. "Play something depressing for us."

Rey nodded once, like he'd file the request away. "I'll see what I can do."

Mara handed him a beer without asking. He stared at it.

"I didn't say I wanted one," he said.

"You didn't have to," she replied. "Stop acting like you're above drinking in a bar you perform in."

"I'm not above it. I'm... tired."

Mara's face softened for half a second. Then she rolled her eyes. "Drink or don't. But you're sitting with us either way."

Rey set the beer down and slid it toward one of her friends. The friend didn't hesitate. Took it like it had been meant for him.

Mara watched Rey's hands. She always did. Like she could tell what was going on in his head by how tight his fingers were around nothing.

"You been sleeping?" she asked, quieter now.

Rey leaned back against the cracked booth and stared past her, letting the noise of the bar fill the answer he didn't want to give.

"A little," he said finally.

Mara hummed like she didn't believe him. "Lidia and Mateo text you?"

"Not yet," Rey said. Then, because he couldn't stop himself, "They're fine."

Mara didn't argue. She just nodded, like she was accepting the statement because it was better than the alternative.

Rey glanced around the bar. A couple at the counter laughed too loud. Someone cursed at the pool table. The bartender wiped the same spot on the counter like it was ritual.

Normal.

It was all normal. And Rey hated how much he wanted it to stay like this.

Mara nudged him with her knee. "You playing tonight or you just here to brood?"

"I said I'd show up," Rey replied.

"That's not what I asked."

Rey looked at her. Really looked. The way her face shifted when she was serious, like she didn't like letting it happen. The way she held her own softness under layers of humor so nobody could grab it.

He'd dated her once. A long time ago. Back when they still thought love had to be romantic to be real.

It had lasted two months. Maybe three. Not long enough to be a story people told, but long enough for them to learn what they needed to learn.

They had kissed. They had tried. They had laid in bed and stared at ceilings and talked about things they weren't ready to say out loud. They had fought once over nothing and then sat in silence and realized the fight wasn't about the argument. It was about the expectation. The idea that if they weren't together like that, then what they were didn't count.

They had ended it with a conversation, not a betrayal. That was rare.

Mara had laughed at the end of it. A small laugh, like relief.

"I love you," she'd said, like it was obvious. "Just not like that."

Rey had nodded, feeling the same thing. "Good. I don't want to lose you trying to force something."

And they never did. Not really.

They became something else. Something sturdier. Like siblings who chose each other in a town where people didn't get to choose much.

Now, sitting across from her, Rey realized he trusted her more than anyone alive. Even his siblings, in a different way. Mara wasn't his responsibility. She was his mirror. The one person who could tell him he was being stupid and he'd actually hear it.

Mara leaned closer, lowering her voice. "I talked to your sister last night."

Rey blinked. "Lidia?"

"Yeah." Mara glanced down at her phone on the table, like she could summon the conversation back. "She texted me. Said she and Mateo might come back early."

Rey's stomach tightened. "Why?"

Mara shrugged, but the shrug didn't carry ease. "She said there were rumors. Like... quarantine talk. Not here. Out there. Colorado."

Rey stared at her. "Quarantine?"

Mara nodded slowly. "She said people on campus were talking. Something about a town. Something about water. She didn't have details. It sounded like... internet panic."

Rey let out a breath, trying to keep it casual. "People always panic."

"Yeah," Mara said. "But Lidia doesn't. Not like that."

Rey's mind flashed through a dozen images—news headlines, old conversations, the Wall in the distance. He didn't connect the dots because he didn't want to. He'd gotten good at that. Ignoring patterns. Pretending threats weren't real until they were standing on his porch.

Mara's voice pulled him back. "She said she wanted to surprise you."

Rey swallowed. "When?"

"Maybe in a couple days," Mara said. "She said she was gonna try to convince Mateo to cut the trip short. Come home. Get her back in time for graduation stuff. She was... excited."

Rey nodded like he was hearing it. Like it was just another normal thing. But the inside of him had shifted, like a floorboard giving way.

He could almost see Lidia's face in his mind. The way she looked when she was trying to pretend she didn't care. The way she acted like she was grown when she still wanted to be taken care of. The way she'd been counting down to graduation like it was a door out of childhood.

"Did she say if they were okay?" Rey asked.

Mara's eyebrows lifted. "Rey. This was last night. Of course they're okay."

He hated himself for asking, and Mara knew it. She reached out and tapped his hand once, quick.

"You're doing that thing," she said.

"What thing?"

"The thing where you act like you don't worry, but you worry so loud it fills the room."

Rey's mouth twitched, almost a smile. "I don't—"

Mara cut him off. "You do."

He leaned back again, letting the noise of the bar cover the moment. Someone behind them shouted for another round. A chair scraped. The jukebox changed songs. A guitar riff started, something old and familiar.

Rey listened to it and felt the smallest ache.

Because this was what he knew. This was his world. Simple in the way it wasn't. A bar, a booth, a friend, a story about his sister coming home.

Mara watched him for a beat, then lifted her chin toward the stage corner where the microphone stood, lonely and waiting.

"You should play," she said.

Rey shook his head. "Not tonight."

"Why?"

He didn't answer. Because the truth was too honest.

Because the quiet in his house that morning had unsettled him, and he didn't know why. Because the Wall had been in his head all week. Because he'd been thinking about writing a song that wasn't ready yet. Because he didn't want to stand under a light while people stared at him like he owed them something.

Mara sighed, then gave him the kind of look she reserved for stubborn children and grown men acting like them.

"Rey," she said, voice low now, real. "You need to be seen."

He stared at her, and the words landed heavier than they should have.

"You disappear too easy," she added. "Even when you're sitting right in front of people."

Rey felt his throat tighten, and he hated it. He hated being understood. He hated how she could pull the truth out of him without touching anything.

He nodded once, a small concession. "Maybe later."

Mara's face softened again, and she let it go, because she knew when to push and when to just stay.

They sat there a while. Talked about nothing. About Lidia's graduation plans. About Mateo complaining about California food. About some guy Mara's friend was dating who sounded like a walking red flag. Rey listened more than he spoke. He laughed once, surprised by it, like the sound didn't belong to him anymore.

At some point, Mara leaned in again and said, almost casually, "If they do come home early... you should let them see you play."

Rey looked at her.

Mara shrugged like it wasn't a big deal, like she wasn't planting something in him on purpose. "Not for the bar crowd. For them. Let your sister see her brother isn't just... the guy who keeps the lights on."

Rey swallowed and looked away, because the thought of it made something in his chest hurt.

He imagined Lidia in the corner of the room, arms crossed, pretending she didn't care, and then slowly uncrossing them as the song turned into something real. Mateo beside her, trying not to look impressed, failing.

He wanted that. More than he wanted anyone else's applause.

He didn't say it.

Instead he tapped his fingers on the table, restless, and said, "I'm working on something."

Mara's eyes lit up, like she'd been waiting for that. "Yeah?"

Rey nodded. "A song. About the Wall."

Mara's face shifted. Just slightly. The humor drained for a second, replaced by something wary.

"The Wall?" she repeated.

Rey nodded again. "It's always there."

Mara stared at him for a beat, then forced the laugh back into her voice like she was sealing something up.

"Write it," she said. "Maybe it'll finally stop staring at you."

Rey didn't laugh.

Because he knew the truth.

The Wall didn't stare.

It waited.

And later—when the pounding came and the lights died and the town poured into the streets like a flood—Rey would remember this booth, this moment, Mara's voice, and the way she said his sister's name like it was a promise.

He would remember it as the last time anything felt normal.

The last time the world gave him a warning soft enough to ignore.

ERADICATION DAY

3

The first shout came from outside.

Not the pounding yet. Just a voice—sharp, amplified, cutting through the neighborhood like it had been dropped there on purpose. Rey was still standing in the kitchen, mug cooling in his hand, when he heard it echo down the street.

"Everyone outside. Now."

The voice didn't sound panicked. That was the part that made his stomach turn. It sounded practiced. Bored, even. Like whoever was saying it had already said it a hundred times and expected to say it a hundred more.

Rey moved to the window and pulled the curtain back an inch.

The street was already filling.

People spilled out of houses half-dressed, some still pulling jackets on, some barefoot on cold pavement. A man across the street yelled at someone who wasn't listening. A woman stood frozen on her porch clutching a phone to her chest like it might start working again if she squeezed hard enough.

Vehicles were parked wrong. Too fast. Doors left open. Engines idling without drivers.

Then he saw the uniforms.

Dark. Padded. Faces hidden behind visors that reflected the sky back at itself. Not local cops. Not state. Something heavier. Something meant to be seen as final.

Rey stepped away from the window and grabbed his guitar, the strap already over his shoulder, bag resting against his hip. His go-bag clipped on like muscle memory. He reached for his phone again. Still nothing. No bars. No service. No emergency alert. Just a dead screen reflecting his own face back at him.

"Come on," he muttered, like the phone could hear him.

It didn't.

A knock rattled the door again—harder now. Closer. Impatient.

Rey opened it.

A uniformed man stood on the porch, weapon held low, visor dark enough that Rey couldn't see his eyes. Behind him, two more moved down the street, knocking, shouting, not stopping.

"Outside," the man said. "Now."

"What's happening?" Rey asked.

The man didn't answer. He took a half-step back and gestured toward the street. The motion was practiced. Efficient.

Rey locked the door behind him out of habit. The click sounded too loud. Like a punctuation mark.

The deputy—soldier—whatever he was—didn't stop him. Just turned and walked, already expecting Rey to follow. Rey did.

The crowd thickened as they moved. People asked questions. No one answered them. A man shouted something about his wife still being inside. Another tried to push back toward his house and was stopped with a hand to his chest. Not rough. Just firm. Final.

The sound of drones built overhead, a layered hum that vibrated in Rey's teeth. He tilted his head back and saw them fanning out, black shapes against the sky, red lights blinking like distant eyes.

They were herding them.

The realization settled in slow and cold.

The Wall rose ahead of them, massive and unavoidable. Rey had seen it from a distance a thousand times, a gray scar on the horizon you learned to ignore if you wanted to keep living. Up close, it felt different. Bigger. Meaner. Like it had been waiting for this moment.

Concrete barriers funneled the crowd toward the main road. Armed personnel lined the sides, bodies rigid now, posture changed. No one was pretending this was temporary anymore.

Someone near Rey started crying. Loud, uncontrolled sobs that cut through the noise. A man snapped at her to stop. She didn't.

Rey's phone vibrated suddenly in his hand.

His heart jumped.

He looked down so fast he nearly dropped it.

Nothing. Just the screen lighting up from the movement. No message. No missed call. Nothing.

He swallowed hard and shoved the phone into his pocket.

That was when a familiar voice cut through the chaos.

"Rey!"

He turned, scanning faces, panic rising—and then he saw her.

Amara pushed through the crowd, elbowing past people twice her size, eyes locked on him like she'd been hunting him. Her hair was pulled back, hoodie half-zipped, breath already short.

"Thank God," she said when she reached him, grabbing his arm like he might vanish. "I couldn't find you."

"Do you know what's going on?" Rey asked.

She shook her head immediately. "No. Nothing. No alerts. No calls. I asked one of the cops and he just told me to keep moving."

Her eyes flicked up toward the drones, then toward the Wall. "I don't think even they know."

They fell into step together, pulled forward by the same current. Rey stayed close to her without thinking about it, like proximity could keep something from happening.

The crowd shifted as they moved, panic rising and falling in waves. Some people shouted. Some prayed. Some stared straight ahead with empty faces, already gone somewhere else.

As they got closer, Rey noticed the scanning towers flanking the opening in the Wall. Tall, angular structures bristling with lights and sensors, sweeping over the line in steady patterns. The air smelled wrong—ozone, dust, fresh-cut concrete.

Inside the Wall, beyond the opening, the city waited.

Vegas rose clean and intact on the other side, glass towers catching the midday sun, neon still glowing faint even in daylight. It looked untouched. Protected. Like nothing bad had ever happened there.

A FEMA encampment sat just inside the threshold—white tents, vehicles parked in neat rows, people in matching vests moving with purpose. Order. Structure.

A murmur rippled through the crowd as people saw it. Relief mixed with confusion.

"They're letting us in," someone said near Rey. "See? We're fine."

Rey didn't feel fine.

The line slowed. Step forward. Pause. Light. Tone. Then waved on.

Rey watched the process with a growing knot in his chest. People passed through the scanners and disappeared into the city. Some smiled when they made it. Some cried. Some just stared.

"What are they scanning for?" Amara whispered.

Rey shook his head. "I don't know."

She leaned closer. "I talked to your sister last night."

The words cut through him sharper than the sirens.

"Lidia?" he asked.

Amara nodded. "She said she and Mateo might come home early. There were rumors. About a quarantine. Somewhere in Colorado."

Rey felt his chest tighten. "When?"

"Soon," Amara said quickly. "In a couple days. They wanted to surprise you."

Too late. The thought came uninvited.

He pictured them on the road. On a campus. Somewhere far away where the sky was still blue and the phones still worked. Somewhere untouched.

"Mateo's with her," Amara added, watching his face. "They're together."

Rey nodded, but his hearing dulled, the world shrinking down to the sound of his own breathing. He reached for his phone again. Still nothing.

Amara's fingers brushed his wrist. "Hey. Stay with me."

A siren wailed behind them.

Then another.

Then a chorus.

The tone shifted instantly. The drones overhead repositioned, their hum deepening into something aggressive. The armed personnel straightened, weapons coming up—not aimed, but ready.

"What's happening?" someone shouted from the back of the line.

The Wall shuddered.

A low mechanical groan rolled through the ground, felt more than heard. Rey turned, dread blooming in his gut, and saw the crowd behind them change all at once.

Panic spread faster than sound.

People pushed. Screamed. Rushed forward. The careful order collapsed into chaos as bodies surged toward the opening. Someone fell. Others tripped over them. Hands reached out, grabbing anything they could.

The doors were moving.

Massive slabs of reinforced steel began sliding inward, slow at first, then faster, the gap narrowing with terrifying inevitability. Alarms flared red across the sky. Drones screamed.

"Move!" someone yelled.

The line disintegrated.

Bodies slammed together, momentum carrying them forward whether they wanted to go or not. Rey felt himself lifted, feet barely touching the ground as the press of people forced him toward the threshold. He lost sight of Amara for a heartbeat, panic spiking—

Then he saw her again. Pale. Eyes wide.

He grabbed her hand.

The sound—he would remember the sound more than anything.

Metal grinding. Flesh hitting steel. A wet, indistinct impact that sent a red mist spraying upward, catching the light before drifting down over screaming faces.

The doors didn't stop.

People were crushed against them, screams cut short as the gap narrowed. Hands clawed at nothing. Someone's shoe came off and vanished beneath the crowd.

Rey was shoved forward, stumbling through the threshold as the doors sealed behind him with a final, echoing slam.

The screams ended.

Silence followed—not true silence, but something close. The drones settled into a steady hover. Survivors stood frozen just inside the Wall, staring back at what wasn't there anymore.

Rey turned slowly.

The Wall stood whole and unbroken, clean as if it had never opened at all. Only red stains marked the seam where the doors met.

His knees gave out.

He dropped to the concrete, the guitar knocking against the ground, strings rattling in protest. His hands shook, useless at his sides. Somewhere nearby, someone retched. Someone else laughed—a thin, broken sound that didn't belong to joy.

Rey looked at the skyline ahead of him, bright and indifferent.

Then he looked back at the Wall.

And understood, with a clarity that burned, that whatever the world had just become, it had decided without him.

And nothing he had been before mattered anymore.

NINE YEARS GONE

4

Nine years passed without permission.

Not in the way people talked about time, like it was a river you floated down until the sharp edges rounded off and everything became tolerable. Rey used to believe that version. The one where grief softened if you just waited long enough. Where the mind got tired of replaying the same horror and eventually filed it away like an old bill you didn't want to pay but had to.

That wasn't how it worked.

Time didn't heal the wound. It just taught his body how to carry it without screaming every second.

The first year after the Wall closed, everything was loud. Not noise-loud. Inside loud. His thoughts crashed into each other. His hands shook at random times. He'd be standing in a line for bread or at a checkpoint while a drone hovered overhead, and suddenly the sound of the Wall grinding shut would slam into his skull so hard he'd flinch like someone hit him.

People noticed then.

They gave him looks. They asked if he was okay. They told him he should talk to somebody. Like there was someone you could talk to who could undo steel slicing through people. Like there was therapy for the sound of a scream being cut off mid-breath.

By year three, people stopped asking.

By year five, they stopped looking.

By year nine, Rey learned how to disappear while standing in the middle of a crowd.

Vegas inside the Boundary wasn't the Vegas people used to talk about.

The old Strip still existed, technically. Some of the buildings still stood like relics. The Luxor still angled into the sky like a black shard, its light cutting upward at night as if it could pierce whatever ceiling the world had built over them. But the city had been reorganized. Controlled. Reinforced. It felt less like a place built for joy and more like a place built to contain it.

Survival had rules now. And rules had enforcers.

The apartment Rey ended up in wasn't what he'd call home. It was a box that kept him from dying in the street. It sat on the wrong side of the Strip, far enough that the bright lights didn't comfort him, close enough that they still invaded his room at night. Neon seeped through the blinds in thin bars, painting his walls in colors that made his skin look sick. Pink. Blue. Green. Sometimes purple, depending on which sign outside decided to flicker harder that week.

The building itself was old in the way no one fixed anything unless it benefited someone important. It creaked when the wind came through the corridors. Pipes knocked in the walls like someone trapped behind them, tapping out an SOS no one answered. The stairwell smelled like old cigarettes and bleach. The elevator broke twice a month and stayed broken long enough you learned to stop checking.

Rey learned the building's sounds the way inmates learned schedules.

Morning meant distant footsteps overhead, neighbors leaving early because whatever work existed inside the Wall demanded it. Midday meant the occasional shout in the hall, someone arguing with someone else, then the abrupt quiet when a patrol drone passed outside and everyone remembered they didn't want attention. Night meant sirens far away, never close enough to help him, always close enough to remind him the city wasn't safe.

Drones were constant.

He heard them more than he saw them—an insect hum that never fully stopped, sometimes fading, sometimes swelling louder as they passed overhead. Rey used to look up. Used to track them with his eyes, trying to understand patterns, trying to reassure himself that if he could predict them he could control something.

Eventually he stopped.

Looking up started to feel like pleading.

The apartment had one main room and a bedroom barely big enough for a bed and a dresser. The kitchen was a corner with a counter that wobbled if you leaned on it too hard. The bathroom fan rattled like it was full of loose screws. The mirror had a crack in one corner that caught the neon light at night and made it look like the room itself was splitting.

Rey didn't decorate.

There wasn't a point.

The guitar leaned in the corner near the couch where it had leaned in his old house, back when his life was defined by routines and siblings and a trust fund that handled the bills even when everything else was chaos. The case was scuffed. The patches were still there—old gigs, old jokes, old places that might as well have been another planet. Dust collected on the strings. The strap hung loose like a slumped shoulder.

He told himself it was temporary.

The first month inside the Wall, he didn't touch it because his fingers wouldn't stop shaking. The second month he didn't touch it because he was tired. By the sixth month, he didn't touch it because he couldn't remember what it felt like to play without hearing screams behind the music.

By the first year, silence became easier.

That was the trap. Silence felt safer because it didn't ask anything of him. It didn't demand his voice. It didn't demand his hands to move. It didn't demand he be present.

The city demanded enough.

He drank at night.

Not every night, at first. Just enough to sleep. Just enough to soften the edges so his mind stopped forcing him back to the threshold of the Wall every time he closed his eyes. There was a point—somewhere between buzzed and numb—where he could pass out without dreaming. He chased that point carefully.

Then he stopped being careful.

Sometimes bottles lined the counter. Sometimes they piled in the trash until the smell got too strong. Sometimes he cleaned them up because he couldn't stand the evidence of himself. He didn't drink in public. He didn't stumble around the streets. He wasn't trying to become a cautionary tale. He drank in the quiet, in the privacy of a room no one cared about, and he called it coping.

He'd never admitted it was drowning.

The day the doors shut stopped being "that day" for everyone else.

It became **Eradication**.

The city named it like naming something meant you owned it. Like if you turned trauma into a proper noun you could file it away under civic history and move on.

Rey didn't say the word.

He didn't need to. The memory lived in his bones. It hit him sometimes in dumb ways—metal grinding when someone dragged a chair across concrete, a sudden slam of a dumpster lid, the hiss of hydraulics at a checkpoint gate. Those sounds weren't the Wall. But his body didn't care. His body heard "closing" and went right back to the seam.

He couldn't remember every face from that day.

He remembered the red mist. The pressure. The way his feet stopped touching the ground as the crowd lifted him, carried him, forced him through the threshold like he was an object. He remembered reaching for Amara's hand and feeling it slip and then finding it again and gripping so hard his fingers hurt.

He remembered thinking, *Lidia and Mateo are out there.*

That thought never left.

It didn't matter how many years passed. It didn't matter how many times he told himself there was nothing he could do. The guilt didn't care about logic. The guilt only cared about one thing: he was inside the Wall, and they were not.

And every day he woke up alive felt like he'd stolen it.

Amara survived the Wall with him.

That alone should've been a blessing. It should've been enough to make the story bearable. The universe had left him at least one person who knew his "before," one person who had been standing beside him when the world turned into a meat grinder.

But blessings came with weight.

Amara didn't let him disappear.

She found him anyway.

The first time she showed up at the apartment, Rey didn't open the door. He sat on the couch, bottle in hand, listening to her knock. Not pounding, not like the evacuation. Just firm. Familiar. Persistent. The kind of knock that said: *I know you're in there.*

He waited for her to leave.

He told himself she would.

She didn't.

He heard her sit down in the hallway, back against the wall. Heard the shift of her jacket. The sigh. The way she settled like she was prepared to stay there all night if she had to.

That was Mara.

She didn't threaten. She didn't beg. She outlasted.

When he finally opened the door, she looked up at him like she'd been waiting the whole time without impatience. Her eyes were tired, but they still held that sharpness he remembered from the dive, from the booth, from the way she could read a room like it was a map.

"You gonna let me in," she asked, voice flat, "or do I need to start yelling your name and explaining this to the neighbors?"

Rey stepped aside.

She walked in like she belonged there, like his apartment was an extension of her responsibility now whether she liked it or not. She didn't comment on the mess. She didn't comment on the bottles. She just looked around once, then looked at him.

"You ate?" she asked.

He shrugged.

She sighed, a sound loaded with disappointment she was trying not to weaponize. "I'll bring something next time."

Next time.

That was how it started. Not with a grand promise. Not with a dramatic scene. Just a sentence that assumed she'd be back.

And she was.

Amara came by after work. After errands. After whatever version of life she'd managed to build inside this controlled, surveilled city. Sometimes she brought food in a paper bag that smelled like fried onions and salt. Sometimes she brought fruit, like she was trying to inject health into him by force. Sometimes she brought nothing but herself and sat in the chair by the window, watching the neon bleed through the blinds while Rey pretended he wasn't watching her.

Some nights she talked. Some nights she didn't. She didn't push him to explain the unexplainable. She didn't ask him how he felt, because she already knew the answer and the answer never changed.

She made sure he ate. She made sure he paid his bills. She reminded him to show up to appointments he didn't care about. She called in favors. She did the small things—mundane, boring, necessary—that kept people alive when they'd decided they didn't deserve to be.

Rey hated that he needed it.

He hated the way it made him feel like a child.

He hated the way he looked forward to her knocking, like a dog waiting for the one person who fed it.

And he hated himself even more for how quickly he got used to it.

At first, he told himself she was doing this because she had nothing else.

That was the lie he used to make it bearable.

Amara had plenty else. She worked. She had friends. She dated. She tried to build a life inside a city that felt like it was still shaking from impact. She wasn't empty.

She just refused to let him rot.

The routine became their relationship. Not romantic. Not even fully spoken. Just a rhythm.

Amara showing up. Rey letting her in.

Somewhere along the line, without anyone deciding it, Amara became his anchor and his caretaker and his witness. She became the person who kept him tethered to humanity.

And that's when it started to break.

Because no one can be someone's life raft forever. Not without drowning too.

The argument didn't feel like it came out of nowhere. It felt like it had been building behind their conversations, behind their silences, for months. Like pressure behind a dam. Like the Wall itself—quiet, looming, waiting.

It happened on a night that looked like any other.

Rey sat on the floor with his back against the couch. Bottle half-empty beside him. The guitar case lay open in front of him, strings slack like the instrument had surrendered. The TV was off. The room was lit by neon leaking through the blinds, painting Amara's face in shifting colors as she stood in the doorway.

She didn't say hi.

She looked at the bottle.

"You didn't eat," she said.

"I'm not hungry."

"You haven't eaten since yesterday."

Rey shrugged, leaning his head back against the couch. "Time's fake."

"Don't," Amara said, sharp.

"Don't what?"

"Don't act like this is clever," she snapped. "It's not. It's just sad."

The word landed heavy.

Rey's jaw tightened. His stomach tightened. Something in him rose up, hot and defensive.

"You don't get to—" he started.

"I do," Amara cut in, voice rising. "I do get to. Because I'm the one who keeps coming back. I'm the one making sure you don't disappear."

Rey laughed once, bitter and small. "You want a medal?"

Amara's face changed. The patience cracked. The exhaustion showed.

"You should've gone with them," Rey said.

The sentence came out before he could stop it, like poison finally finding the opening.

Amara froze.

"What?" she whispered.

"That night," Rey continued, words spilling fast, fueled by alcohol and guilt and years of rot. "When you talked to Lidia. When you knew about the quarantine rumor. You should've told them not to come back. You should've made them stay in California. You could've stopped this."

Amara's eyes flashed, then filled, then hardened.

"You think I don't replay that?" she shouted. "You think I don't hear her voice every time I close my eyes? You think I don't wonder if one different word could've changed everything?"

Rey stood up unsteady, the room tilting slightly. "Then why are you still here?"

The question hung between them like a slap.

Amara blinked, jaw clenched. She wiped at her face hard, angry at the tears.

"Because I love you," she said, voice breaking. "And I can't watch you kill yourself."

"I'm not dead," Rey snapped.

"You're not living either," she shot back. "You're stuck. You're frozen on that day and you keep dragging me into it."

The words hurt because they were true.

"I can't care for you like a child," Amara continued. "I want you alive, Rey. Not preserved. Not surviving. Alive."

Rey opened his mouth. Nothing came out.

Amara shook her head like she was trying to shake the hope out too, because hope was what kept breaking her.

"Your siblings would want you to play," she said. "They'd want you to be more than this. You think Lidia would want you sitting on the floor with a bottle?"

Rey's throat tightened at her name.

Amara grabbed her jacket.

"Find me when you're ready," she said, voice quieter now, exhausted. "When you want to stop being broken."

Then she left.

The door closed behind her with a sound that felt permanent.

Rey didn't chase her.

He stood in the neon light and stared at the door like it might open again if he stared hard enough. Like he could rewind the last ten minutes. Like he could swallow the poison back down.

He couldn't.

The first day after she left, he didn't drink.

Not as some grand statement. He just... couldn't. The bottle sat there and he stared at it and felt nothing. No comfort. No pull. Just emptiness.

The second day, he drank twice as much.

The third day, he sat on the edge of the bed with the bottle in his hand and didn't open it.

Instead, he cleaned.

Slowly. Methodically. Like he was following orders. Bottles in the trash. Dishes in the sink. Clothes folded, even though no one would ever see them. The apartment felt wrong without the mess, like he'd erased evidence of his decay.

When he finished, he sat on the floor and stared at the guitar.

It stared back.

He tightened the strings.

His fingers hurt immediately. Calluses gone soft from neglect. The sound that came out when he strummed was uneven, unfamiliar, like the guitar didn't trust him yet.

He played anyway.

Not loud. Not well. Just enough to feel the vibration travel up his arm and remind him he was still capable of making something other than damage.

He stopped. Started again. Found a chord. Let it ring. Let it die.

And in that small, quiet act, something shifted.

Not healed. Not fixed.

But moved.

The next night, he went to a bar.

Not to drink.

Just to play.

He didn't tell himself it was a comeback. He didn't tell himself it meant anything. He just put the guitar on his back and walked into a room full of noise and took a breath like he was stepping into weather.

And for the first time in nine years, the silence didn't feel empty.

It felt like it was waiting.

THE SONG

5

R ey didn't go back to the bar right away.

He told himself it was timing. That he needed to let his fingers heal. That the soreness crawling up his forearms was a sign he'd rushed it, that the guitar deserved patience. Those explanations sounded responsible when he thought them through, even convincing, like they were decisions instead of fear wearing better clothes.

The truth was simpler and heavier.

He was afraid the silence would leave.

Not the kind of silence he'd lived in for years—the hollow, padded quiet of his apartment at night when the city's hum softened just enough to let him sleep. He knew that silence. He'd trained himself to survive in it. This was different.

This was a listening silence.

The kind that leaned toward him when he touched the strings. The kind that made the room feel occupied even when he was alone. The kind that asked something back.

He didn't trust it.

The days after Amara left stretched in an uncomfortable way, like time had lost its sense of proportion. The apartment stayed clean now. Not immaculate—just deliberate. The absence of clutter made everything sharper. Without bottles to kick aside or dishes to avoid, there was nowhere for his eyes to rest without landing on memory.

Without alcohol blurring the edges, things came back wrong.

Not the Wall. Not at first. Smaller moments. Lidia's voice drifting down the hallway when she thought he wasn't listening. Mateo tapping rhythms on the dashboard while Rey drove, turning traffic into percussion. The way Amara used to sit on the arm of the couch and steal fries off his plate without asking, like the boundary had never existed between them.

Those memories didn't scream.

They waited.

On the fourth night, he stood in the kitchen with his hand hovering over the cabinet.

The bottle sat inside like a promise. Like it had learned the shape of his weakness and adjusted itself accordingly. Just one drink, he told himself. Not to disappear. Just to take the edge off. Just to sleep.

He closed his eyes and leaned his forehead against the cabinet door, breathing slow through his nose, trying to remember the sound of Amara's voice when she said she wanted him alive. Not preserved. Alive.

He opened the cabinet.

Stared at the bottle.

Then closed it again.

The click sounded louder than it should've. Like a decision echoing in a room that hadn't heard one in a long time.

Rey grabbed the guitar instead.

It felt heavier than he remembered. Or maybe his arms were weaker. Maybe both things were true. He sat on the edge of the couch and rested the body against his thigh, adjusting the strap until it stopped cutting into his shoulder. His fingers hovered over the strings without touching them, like he was waiting for permission.

He strummed once.

The sound came out uneven. A little sour. He winced and adjusted the tuning peg, listening carefully as the note settled. He played again. Better. Not clean. But closer.

His fingers remembered more than he thought they would.

Calluses softened by neglect complained immediately, but the pain felt honest. Earned. He let it happen. Played through it. Let the muscle memory wake up slowly, like something coming out of hibernation.

He didn't try to write.

Not at first.

He played fragments. Chords without direction. Pieces of old progressions he never finished. Songs he'd abandoned years ago because they didn't say what he needed them to say. He stopped and started again, frustrated, patient, then frustrated again.

At some point, without meaning to, he started humming.

Not words. Just sound. Low and quiet. Testing the space.

The melody arrived sideways.

Not as a complete thought. Not as inspiration. Just a line he'd been carrying around for years without realizing it had weight. He played it once. Then again. Changed a chord. Slowed the tempo. Let it breathe.

He reached for the notebook he hadn't opened since before Eradication.

The cover stuck slightly, like it had resisted being remembered. Pages crackled as he flipped through, past old lyrics that belonged to another life. Love songs that felt naïve now. Anger songs that didn't know what real anger was yet. Notes about gigs and reminders to call venues that no longer existed.

He found a blank page.

Stared at it.

The first line didn't come easy.

When it did, it hurt.

He wrote it anyway.

Crossed it out.

Wrote it again differently.

Scratched that out too.

The song fought him—not because it didn't want to exist, but because it demanded precision. Honesty without poetry. Truth without protection.

He wrote until his wrist cramped and his eyes burned. He played until his fingers went numb. He lost track of time completely, caught in the loop of write-play-rewrite, chasing something he could feel but not quite touch.

When the sun started bleeding through the blinds, he stopped.

The song wasn't finished.

But it was awake.

That night, he walked past the bar without going in.

The neon sign buzzed overhead, familiar and indifferent. Music spilled out when the door opened for someone else, laughter following it into the street. Rey slowed, stood there a moment, then kept walking.

He wasn't ready.

The next night, he stood in the doorway and listened.

The place hadn't changed. Same smell of old beer and fryer grease. Same bartender wiping the same spot on the counter like repetition was a form of prayer. A band played covers loud enough to drown out conversation. People shouted lyrics they barely remembered, nostalgia doing most of the work.

Rey stayed for one song.

Then left.

He went home and kept writing.

The third night, he brought the guitar inside.

No announcement. No confidence. He took a seat near the edge of the room, back to the wall, the case at his feet like a security blanket. He waited while the band finished their set, hands folded loosely in his lap, pulse steady enough to pass for calm.

He didn't order a drink.

Didn't talk to anyone.

He waited.

The bartender noticed him eventually. Squinted through the dim light.

"You playing," the bartender asked, "or you just haunting the place?"

Rey shrugged. "Haven't decided."

The bartender snorted. "Same as always."

When the band packed up and the room shifted into that loose, in-between state—half restless, half drunk—Rey stood.

He didn't ask for the mic.

He didn't clear his throat or make a joke to warm the room.

He stepped into the light like he'd done it a hundred times before and adjusted the stand until it felt right. Familiar. Grounded.

The room didn't quiet immediately.

People talked. Glasses clinked. Someone laughed too loud. Rey waited. Let the noise exist. Let the room decide if it wanted to listen.

He strummed once.

Soft.

Let the sound hang there like a question.

Then he played.

The song moved slow and deliberate. A soft rock ballad stripped of anything flashy. No big hook. No dramatic build. Just a steady progression that carried the weight without rushing it. The words came out careful at first, then stronger as he trusted them not to betray him.

He didn't name Eradication.

He didn't need to.

The loss lived between the lines. In the pauses. In the way his voice dropped on certain words. In the way the melody refused to resolve cleanly.

Halfway through the first verse, the room changed.

Conversation tapered. Chairs stopped scraping. A woman near the bar lowered her glass and didn't lift it again. Someone sniffed, sharp and surprised, like the emotion had caught them off guard.

Rey didn't look up.

He focused on the strings. On the rhythm. On keeping his voice steady when it wanted to break.

When the chorus came, he felt it land.

Not like applause. Like recognition.

People leaned forward without realizing it. The room held its breath.

When the song ended, there was a pause.

Not applause.

Stillness.

Then one clap. Slow. Careful. Another followed. Then more. The sound built, but it wasn't wild. It wasn't celebration.

It was acknowledgment.

Rey nodded once, more to himself than anyone else, and stepped back.

The bartender met him halfway.

"You can play here anytime," he said quietly. "I'll pay you. And I know a couple people at local stations. They're looking for something real."

Rey shook his head. "I don't want money."

The bartender studied him for a moment, then nodded. "Figures. Still—people need this. You gave them a voice tonight."

Rey didn't answer.

As he packed up, a woman approached him. Older. Hispanic. Hair pulled back. Eyes dark and sharp with emotion she hadn't bothered to hide.

She touched his arm lightly, like asking permission.

"Tu eres el rey," she said softly. "De la gente."

Rey blinked. "What?"

The bartender translated from behind him, faint smile tugging at his mouth. "She says you're the king of the people."

Rey felt something twist in his chest. "I'm not—"

"I know," the woman said in accented English, shaking her head gently. "That's why."

She walked away before he could respond.

Rey stood there longer than necessary, guitar in hand, the words settling over him like weight he hadn't asked for. King implied power. Control. Authority.

He had none of those things.

He left the bar before anyone could say anything else.

Outside, the streets glowed neon and artificial, the city humming with life that felt disconnected from him. He walked fast, heart pounding, like he was late for something he didn't understand yet.

Amara's words echoed in his head.

You need to be seen.

He turned the corner onto her street.

The neon vanished.

Red and blue lights replaced it, flashing hard enough to wash the color out of everything else. Police cruisers lined the curb. Yellow tape stretched across a yard he recognized instantly.

Her house.

Rey stopped.

Then ran.

The rest would come fast.

Too fast.

And by the time the night ended, the song would no longer belong only to him.

It would belong to the broken.

EL REY

6

The name didn't arrive all at once.

It didn't explode into the city with posters or whispers carried by rumor networks or someone clever enough to brand it. It slipped in quietly, the way things that mattered always did. Through mouths that didn't realize they were passing it on. Through rooms that didn't know they were changing shape around it.

Rey heard it first the way you heard weather before you felt it.

A pause in conversation when he walked into a bar he'd never played before. A glance that lingered a second too long. Someone nudging someone else and leaning in close, voices dropping even though he was still too far away to hear them.

He ignored it.

That had become a skill.

The second time he heard it, it came from behind him.

He was packing up after a set—same ritual, same care—when a voice near the back door said it quietly, almost reverently, like it wasn't meant for him at all.

"El Rey."

Rey paused, fingers still on the zipper of the guitar case. He didn't turn around. Didn't ask who said it or what they meant. He finished packing like he hadn't heard anything, slung the strap over his shoulder, and walked out into the night before anyone could make it real.

He told himself it didn't matter.

He told himself names were just noise.

But the city remembered things differently than people did.

The next night, he played somewhere else. A smaller place. Dirtier. The kind of bar that didn't bother pretending it was anything other than what it was. He showed up late, waited his turn, stepped into the light without introduction.

The room quieted faster this time.

Not immediately. Not magically. Just... sooner. Like the sound recognized him before the people did.

He played the song again.

It landed heavier.

Not because he changed it. Not because he sang it better. The words were the same. The chords were the same. But the room was different. The people were different. Their grief had different shapes. Different edges. The song bent around them and came back altered.

Rey felt it happen and didn't know what to do with it.

After the set, a man approached him near the bar. Mid-forties. Work boots scuffed white at the toes. Hands rough, knuckles thick with old scars like he'd spent a lifetime fixing things that didn't want to be fixed.

The man didn't introduce himself.

"My wife didn't make it," he said, staring at the floor between them.

Rey didn't answer. He didn't ask questions. He'd learned those were dangerous when people started with a sentence like that.

"She was behind me," the man continued, voice steady in a way that scared Rey more than tears would've. "I turned around to grab her hand and she was just... gone."

The man swallowed hard. His jaw worked like he was chewing something bitter.

"I haven't talked about it," he said. "Not really. Didn't know how."

Rey nodded once. Slow. Careful. Like he was acknowledging a truth that didn't need commentary.

The man reached into his pocket and pulled out a folded bill, pressed it into Rey's hand.

Rey shook his head immediately. "I don't—"

"Take it," the man said, finally looking at him. His eyes were red, rimmed with exhaustion that went deeper than sleep. "It's not for you. It's for her."

Rey closed his fingers around the bill.

He didn't say thank you.

The man didn't wait for it.

Rey tucked the money into the guitar case and left it there, untouched, like a marker. Like proof that something had passed between them that wasn't transactional.

It didn't stop there.

A woman stopped him on the sidewalk one night, just outside the glow of a flickering sign. She didn't cry. She didn't even look particularly sad. She just said, "My brother used to sing," and then thanked him like he'd returned something she thought she'd lost for good.

A bartender poured him water without asking and set it down in front of him like it was the most natural thing in the world. "On the house," she said. "You're doing enough."

People started showing up early when they heard he might play.

Not crowds. Not lines. Just… more people than usual. People who stayed longer. People who didn't drink as much. People who sat closer to the stage without realizing they were doing it.

Rey didn't change his routine.

He didn't promote. He didn't announce. He didn't build a setlist. He played the song when it felt right, sometimes first, sometimes last, sometimes not at all. He trusted the room more than he trusted himself.

The name followed anyway.

"El Rey."

Sometimes it was spoken with warmth. Sometimes with gratitude. Sometimes with something close to desperation, like the speaker needed it to be true.

Rey hated that part.

He didn't want to be what people leaned on. He didn't want to be elevated. He didn't want the responsibility that came with being named anything larger than human.

He was tired of roles.

He was tired of surviving other people's expectations.

One night, after a set that left the room so quiet it felt like pressure, the bartender from the first bar leaned against the counter and watched him pack up.

"They're calling you El Rey now," the bartender said casually, like he was commenting on the weather.

Rey didn't look up. "They shouldn't."

The bartender shrugged. "They don't mean it like you think."

Rey zipped the case shut and finally met his eyes. "What does that mean?"

The bartender considered him for a moment, then nodded toward the empty stools and half-cleared glasses. "You don't rule anything," he said. "You don't tell anyone what to do. You don't lead marches or give speeches."

He paused, letting the words settle.

"You just stand there and say the thing they don't know how to say yet."

Rey swallowed.

"That's not a king," Rey said.

The bartender smiled faintly. "Exactly."

Outside, the city hummed. Drones passed overhead, their lights blinking steady and indifferent. Neon signs buzzed and flickered, selling distraction the way they always had. Somewhere deeper inside the Wall, music blasted louder and cleaner and emptier, polished to the point of meaninglessness.

Rey walked home instead of taking the bus.

He liked feeling the ground under his feet. Liked knowing where he was in relation to everything else. He took the same routes over and over until they became familiar enough to stop thinking about. Past shuttered storefronts with papered windows. Past checkpoints that barely glanced at him anymore, his face filed away as harmless, unthreatening.

Sometimes people recognized him.

They didn't approach. Not usually. They nodded. Touched their chest once. Looked away.

Rey nodded back.

Gratitude made him uncomfortable. It felt heavier than grief. Like something he could drop if he wasn't careful.

At home, the apartment stayed clean now. Not sterile. Lived-in. The bottles were gone. The cabinet stayed closed, though some nights he still stood in front of it longer than necessary, fingers resting on the handle, reminding himself that wanting something didn't mean he had to take it.

The guitar lived closer to him now.

Not in the corner. Not leaning away. It rested within arm's reach of the couch, like a presence he acknowledged daily. He wrote more. Not just about Eradication. About mornings. About hands. About the way people stayed when leaving would've been easier. About the way people left because staying would've destroyed them.

Some songs never left the notebook. Some were too raw to touch twice. Some made him stop mid-line and stare at the wall, chest tight, waiting for the feeling to pass.

He never wrote about Amara directly.

He didn't need to.

She lived in the pauses. In the way his voice softened on certain words. In the way he always hesitated before starting a song, like he was checking if she was in the room.

One night, after a set, a young woman waited until the bar emptied before approaching him. She couldn't have been more than twenty. She held her jacket tight around her like armor.

"My brother used to play," she said. "He died on Eradication Day."

Rey nodded.

"I don't remember his songs anymore," she said. "But when you played tonight... I felt him. Just for a second."

Rey closed the case slowly, careful with the zipper like it might break.

"That's enough," he said.

She smiled through tears and left without another word.

Later, alone in the apartment, Rey sat on the floor with his back against the couch, guitar resting across his lap. The city's glow pressed in through the blinds, painting the room in restless color. He thought about the Wall. About the way it closed. About the people it took.

He thought about how the city had named the day and moved on.

And he thought about the name they'd given him.

El Rey.

Not a ruler.

Not a savior.

Just someone who stayed long enough to listen.

Rey rested his forehead against the body of the guitar and closed his eyes.

If this was the shape his life had taken—

if this was what remained when everything else was stripped away—

then he would carry it carefully.

Not as a crown.

As a burden.

As a promise.

Tomorrow night, he would play again.

BROKEN

7

Rey didn't remember deciding to go to Amara's.

He remembered the streets.

He remembered the way the city looked when you walked fast enough that the neon stopped being pretty and started being a warning. Signs bled color across wet pavement. Blue and pink reflections stretched and warped under his boots. The air smelled like exhaust and fried food and something electrical, like the city was always one bad spark away from darkness.

He remembered the guitar case hitting his side with every step. A steady thump-thump that kept time with his heartbeat. Like the instrument was reminding him it was real. Like it was keeping him from floating away.

He remembered thinking, *I need to tell her.*

Not that he'd played. Not that people listened. Not even that they called him El Rey.

He needed to tell her he was trying.

That she hadn't wasted her time pulling him up all those years.

That he heard her. That he'd finally heard her.

The words ran in his head as he moved—simple ones, stupid ones, the kind you didn't rehearse unless you were scared you'd never get the chance.

Mara, I'm sorry.

Mara, I played.

Mara, I didn't drink.

Mara, you were right.

He turned down her street and felt it before he saw it.

The air changed.

Noise tightened. Conversations got smaller. The city's hum shifted into a different frequency, the kind that made your neck tense even if you didn't know why. Then the red and blue lights hit the buildings ahead, flashing hard enough to erase the neon for a second at a time.

Police.

Rey slowed like his body had made the decision without him. The guitar strap dug into his shoulder as he stopped mid-step. A patrol car sat crooked at the curb, driver door open. Another was behind it, lights strobing, reflecting off windows and turning the street into a pulsing tunnel.

Uniforms moved in controlled patterns. Yellow tape stretched across a yard he recognized instantly. A house with a porch light that used to flicker. A front step he'd stood on a hundred times. A place that smelled like cheap candles and laundry detergent and whatever Mara had cooked last time she let him sit at her table without making him talk.

Her house.

His throat closed.

Rey took a step forward.

A uniformed officer shifted immediately, body turning toward him notifying the detective he was speaking with. Hand lifting in a stop gesture.

"Sir, you can't—"

"That's my friend," Rey said, voice too loud, too thin. "Amara. She lives there."

The officer hesitated, eyes scanning Rey like he was trying to decide if this was grief or a problem. Then another man stepped away from the cluster near the porch. Taller. Broad shoulders. Detective button down. Hair cut short but a little unkempt. Face tired in the way people got when they'd seen too much and still had to keep looking at it. He too was searching for something, somewhere.

He walked toward Rey with measured calm, like he'd done this conversation before.

"Hey," the detective said, one hand held up, not aggressive, just controlling space. "Take a breath. What's your name?"

Rey swallowed. "Rey."

"Last name?"

Rey blinked, like the detail didn't matter, like his identity had been reduced to one word for so long he'd forgotten the rest. "Alvarez," he said. "Rey Alvarez."

The detective nodded once trying to match and respect him. "Detective Bill Wilkins."

The name hit Rey with a weird kind of recognition. Not because he knew him, but because he'd heard it. Around the city. In conversations that stopped when you walked into the wrong room. The kind of name that carried authority without needing volume.

Wilkins looked past Rey briefly, checking the street, then back. His eyes were steady. Not cold. Just professional, and that somehow made it worse.

"Rey," Wilkins said, slower now, "what are you doing here tonight?"

Rey's mouth opened. Nothing came out clean.

"I... I was coming to see her," he managed. "I needed to talk to her."

Wilkins held Rey's gaze for a moment longer than necessary, like he was reading something on his face. Then he nodded toward the sidewalk. A small step away from the flashing lights. A small step away from the tape.

"Come over here," Wilkins said. "Let's talk." He motioned away from other officers and forensic people marching along doing their jobs.

Rey moved like his joints were stiff. Like his body was heavier than it should've been. He stopped where Wilkins pointed, near a streetlight that flickered occasionally, like even the infrastructure couldn't handle too much truth at once.

Rey stared at the porch.

He half-expected Mara to step out and wave like it was nothing. Like she'd planned this. Like she'd orchestrated the scene just to scare him into showing up.

She didn't.

Wilkins took a breath, the kind people took right before saying something they didn't want to say.

"There was a call," Wilkins said. "Reported robbery in progress. Units responded. When they arrived, they found two victims inside."

Rey didn't understand the words as a sentence. They came in pieces. Robbery. Units. Victims.

He stared at Wilkins' mouth like maybe he'd misheard.

"Amara Torres?" Rey asked, even though he already knew. "Is she—"

Wilkins' jaw tightened subtly. "Yes."

The street seemed to tilt.

Rey's hand tightened around the guitar strap, knuckles whitening. He didn't realize he'd been holding his breath until he exhaled and it shook.

"No," Rey said. It came out as a whisper at first. Then louder, angry. "No. That doesn't— She's not—"

Wilkins didn't flinch. He'd seen denial before. He waited until Rey's voice ran out of fuel.

"She and her boyfriend were killed," Wilkins said, voice low enough to feel almost respectful. "Suspect fled before patrol made entry."

Rey stared at the porch again.

Boyfriend. Right. Mara had tried. She'd built something, while he didn't. Even with the city broken and everyone carrying grief like a second skin, she'd still tried to make a life. Rey had known about the boyfriend, but he'd never cared about the details minus the occasions he'd buy him drinks the few times they did go out together. Not because he didn't care about her happiness—because the part of him that loved her like family didn't need to compete with anybody.

Now the word sat in the air like an accusation.

"Mara... she's dead," Rey said, like repeating it would make it less impossible.

Wilkins nodded once. "Yes."

Rey's mouth went dry. His tongue felt thick.

"What happened?" he asked. "Who did it?"

Wilkins glanced toward the street where drones hovered in the distance like insects. "We believe it was a targeted burglary. Opportunistic. Not personal."

The words didn't help.

Nothing about Mara's life felt opportunistic. She wasn't careless. She didn't leave doors unlocked. She didn't walk alone in dark alleys.

She didn't do stupid things. She was the one who survived by paying attention.

"How does a burglary—" Rey started, voice rising, then cracking. "How does a burglary end with—"

Wilkins' face tightened again, not with impatience, but with the weight of answering the same question that never had a satisfying answer.

"The suspect panicked," Wilkins said. "It escalated. When drones pinged him in the area, he knew units would arrive. He took his own life a few blocks away before we could take him into custody."

Rey blinked.

"So... that's it?" he said. "He just—"

"He's dead," Wilkins confirmed. "Yes."

No trial. No explanation. No motive you could hold in your hands and shake until it made sense. Just an ending, abrupt and pointless, like a door slamming.

Rey swallowed hard and looked at the tape again. Yellow line separating what had happened from what was still happening. Like the city could draw boundaries around grief and keep it contained.

His stomach rolled.

He turned slightly, away from Wilkins, and breathed through his nose, slow, like he was trying not to throw up on the sidewalk.

A laugh escaped somewhere down the street—someone not involved, someone passing by, someone living. The sound didn't belong in this moment. It felt obscene. Rey's hands shook.

Wilkins spoke again, softer now, and Rey realized the detective had shifted from information to something almost human.

"Did you have family you can call?" Wilkins asked.

Rey almost laughed. Almost. The sound got stuck in his throat.

"My family is gone," Rey said. He didn't mean his blood family. Or maybe he did. He didn't know anymore. "My siblings... they were supposed to come back. Years ago."

Wilkins perked to ask a question he initially was hesitant too. "Do you know if she had any ties with The Remnant group?"

In a daze couldn't muster any knowledge. "Nothing with those... mobs."

A quiet moment. Why the Remnant... An anarchist group. They believe in a cure to bring the walls down and do violence. Mara. No. How dare he ask.

Wilkins' eyes flicked to the guitar case, sensing the tension and hoping to descalate. Recognition did hit in time. "You're the musician."

Rey blinked. "What?"

Wilkins nodded toward the case like it explained everything. "You've been playing around town. People talk. I've been to bar or two also."

Rey didn't respond. The idea that the city had been speaking his name while he'd been standing here about to lose Mara felt like a cruel joke.

Wilkins held Rey's gaze a second longer. Then, with the same controlled calm he'd approached with, he said, "I'm sorry, Rey."

It was the closest thing to comfort the city offered.

Rey nodded once, small and stiff, like if he moved too much he would fall apart.

He didn't say goodbye.

He didn't ask to see her.

He didn't ask anything else at all.

He turned and walked away.

Not because he didn't care.

Because if he stayed one more second he wasn't sure he'd survive it.

The walk back to his apartment didn't feel like distance.

It felt like he'd stepped out of time.

The neon returned as he left Mara's street, but it looked wrong now. Artificial. Insulting. The city kept flashing colors at him like it expected him to keep playing the game, keep moving, keep consuming distractions.

He kept walking.

People passed him. A couple arguing. A group laughing. A man pushing a cart full of scrap. A woman smoking outside a closed storefront, eyes half-lidded and distant. Nobody looked at Rey. Nobody knew what had just been ripped out of him.

He hated them for it, then hated himself for hating them.

He made it to the apartment building and climbed the stairs because the elevator had been broken for months and no one fixed anything unless it benefited someone important. His boots hit each step like counting down to something he didn't want to reach.

Inside, the apartment was quiet.

Not peaceful quiet.

The kind of quiet that pressed in.

Rey set the guitar down by the couch like he always did. He stared at it for a long time, then looked away like it had offended him by still existing.

He didn't sit at first.

He moved around the room like a machine.

Picked up a cup from the counter and put it in the sink. Straightened a chair that didn't need straightening. Folded a blanket he hadn't used. He didn't know why he was doing it. His hands just needed something to do that wasn't shaking.

His eyes landed on the cabinet.

He walked to it.

Opened it.

The bottle sat there like it had been waiting for him. Like it had heard the news before he did. Like it knew exactly what it was for.

Rey stared at it.

His hand reached.

He stopped.

He thought of Mara's face when she told him she couldn't keep caring for him like a child. The way her voice broke. The way she still said she loved him anyway. He thought of the last words she'd left him with.

Find me when you're ready.

He exhaled hard and shut the cabinet.

The sound echoed in the small kitchen like a decision.

Rey sat down on the floor, back against the couch, knees bent, hands resting uselessly on his thighs. The apartment felt too clean and too empty at the same time. Like it didn't know whether it was a home or a holding cell.

He stared at the wall across from him. Neon bled through the blinds and made the paint look bruised.

His phone sat on the coffee table. Dead. Still dead. Like it always was when it mattered.

He didn't cry.

Not at first.

His body didn't know what to do with grief anymore. It had spent too long swallowing it. Storing it. Letting it rot inside him until it became part of him.

He thought of the first time Mara showed up at his apartment nine years ago. Sitting in the hallway like she owned the space. Refusing to leave. He thought of the booth at the dive, her voice saying his sister's name. He thought of how she'd called him dramatic, how she'd pushed him back into the world like she was physically hauling him by the collar.

And then the images switched, cruel and fast.

Her house. Tape. Flashing lights. Wilkins' mouth forming words that didn't fit reality.

Rey's throat tightened. His eyes burned. He pressed the heels of his hands into his face, hard, like he could push the grief back inside.

It didn't go.

He took the guitar into his lap.

The wood felt cool against his forearm. Familiar. Solid.

He didn't play right away.

He just held it.

He sat there a long time, breathing through the tightness in his chest, listening to the city outside pretend it was normal.

Then his fingers moved.

Not a chord. Not a song. Just a single note.

It rang out soft and clean, cutting through the quiet like a thread.

Rey swallowed and whispered, "I'm sorry."

The words weren't to Mara's spirit or God or anyone listening.

They were to the air. To the apartment. To himself.

His fingers found another note. Then another. A progression, slow and heavy, like walking through mud. The melody came first, dragging something behind it. Rey didn't chase it like a musician trying to write. He followed it like a man trying to find his way out of a dark room.

And then the words arrived.

Not all at once. Not polished. Not poetic.

Honest.

The first line hit him like a confession.

You found me broken on the floor that night...

His voice cracked on the first attempt. He stopped. Breathed. Tried again, softer, letting the words sit in his mouth before releasing them.

He saw it as he sang—Mara standing in his doorway, arms crossed, eyes tired. The bottle beside him. His shame. Her anger. Her love anyway.

Empty bottles, empty eyes, no fight left inside...

The line hurt because it wasn't exaggeration. It was record.

He kept going.

Pulled me up when I couldn't stand...

His fingers shook, but the chords stayed steady, like the guitar was doing the holding for him.

He paused after the first verse, staring down at the strings, waiting for the urge to stop. Waiting for the voice in his head to tell him this was stupid, this was too much, this was embarrassing, this was too real.

Instead, he heard Mara's voice.

You need to be seen.

He kept writing.

The chorus came with a weight that made his chest tighten so hard he thought he might choke.

I miss you more than words can say...

He had to swallow between lines.

He had to stop once and press his forehead against the guitar's body, eyes closed, breathing shallow, letting the wave pass.

Then he wrote again.

He wrote like he was bleeding something out so it wouldn't poison him.

You were the light in my darkest storm...

The words weren't clever. They weren't trying to impress anyone. They were the kind of words a man wrote when he had nothing left to hide behind.

He kept seeing her hands. The way she touched his wrist in the crowd at the Wall. The way she tapped his hand in the booth. The way she shoved him back into the world, again and again, refusing to let him vanish.

And now she was gone.

And the world had taken her the same way it had taken everything else.

Not with meaning.

With force.

He wrote the bridge last.

It came out quieter than the rest, like a final truth he didn't want to admit.

If I could trade these scars for one more day...

His vision blurred. He blinked hard, angry at his eyes for doing what they were supposed to do.

He finished the last line and let the final chord ring.

The sound hung in the room a moment, then faded into the city's distant hum.

Rey didn't move.

He didn't clap. He didn't feel relief.

He felt hollow.

But in the hollow, something else existed too. Something small. Something steady.

A vow.

Not a heroic vow. Not a cinematic one.

A simple one.

He would play.

He would stand in front of strangers and give them the words they didn't have. He would let the city name him if it needed to. Not because he wanted a crown, but because people were drowning and sound was one of the last things that could pull them back to the surface.

He would play for the ones crushed behind the Wall.

He would play for Lidia and Mateo, wherever their ghosts lived.

He would play for Mara.

He would play for the broken.

Rey looked down at the guitar and tightened his grip around the neck, like he was holding onto a living thing.

Outside, the neon kept buzzing. The drones kept patrolling. The city kept pretending it was fine.

Inside, Rey sat in the quiet with the song in his hands.

And for the first time since Eradication, he didn't feel like disappearing.

He felt like showing up.

FOR THE PEOPLE

EPILOGUE

No one knew where he lived.

That was the first rumor.

Some said he stayed near the old Strip, tucked into one of the buildings everyone avoided because the elevators never worked and the lights flickered even when the grid was stable. Others said he moved constantly, never sleeping in the same place twice, drifting between neighborhoods like sound carried on air. A few swore he lived outside the Wall, that he crossed back and forth through service gates no one else could access, playing for people the city pretended weren't there.

None of it was true.

None of it needed to be.

Rey learned early that the city didn't need facts. It needed shapes. It needed stories that fit around the damage without touching it directly. When people couldn't explain how they survived something, they explained it by attaching meaning to whoever stood closest to the feeling.

That was how myths formed now. Quietly. Functionally.

Rey didn't correct anyone.

He played where he was asked, when it felt right. Not every night. Not even every week. He learned to listen to his body again, to recognize when the weight was too heavy and when it could be carried. Some nights he turned invitations down without explanation. Other nights he showed up unannounced and left before anyone could thank him.

He never took the same path twice if he could help it.

Not because he was hiding.

Because repetition turned things into routine, and routine was how the city learned to own things.

Bars changed after he played there.

Not visibly. Not in ways inspectors or administrators would notice. But the noise shifted. The volume dipped earlier in the night. People drank slower. Sometimes they talked less. Sometimes they talked more, but quieter, like they didn't want to break something fragile.

Once, Rey walked past a bar he'd played months earlier and heard someone inside singing one of his lines wrong. The melody was off. The words weren't exact. It should've bothered him.

It didn't.

The song didn't belong to him anymore.

He saw it happen in smaller ways too.

A bartender who used to drown every shift in alcohol started pouring water between drinks, unprompted. A man who never spoke about Eradication began telling a story about his sister like it was allowed now. A woman brought her father to a show because he "needed to hear something that didn't lie to him."

Rey learned to accept gratitude without absorbing it.

That was the hardest part.

People wanted to thank him like he'd done something extraordinary. Like he'd saved them. Like he'd pulled them back from the edge when the truth was simpler and harder to explain.

He had just stayed.

The city had spent years teaching people how to look away. How to normalize walls and drones and names for mass death. How to call survival "progress" and loss "necessary."

Rey didn't argue with any of it.

He just stood in front of people and refused to look away.

Sometimes, that was enough.

There were nights when the Wall felt closer.

Those nights came without warning. The air felt heavier. The hum of drones seemed louder. Conversations ended sooner. People glanced toward the horizon even when they were deep inside the city.

On those nights, Rey didn't play Eradication.

He played something softer. Something almost hopeful, though he'd never have called it that. Songs about hands finding each other in the dark. About people choosing to stay even when staying hurt. About mornings that came anyway.

Once, someone asked him why he didn't play the song everyone knew him for.

Rey thought about it for a long moment before answering.

"Because that song reminds people of what they lost," he said. "Sometimes they need to remember what's still here."

No one argued.

The name followed him whether he wanted it to or not.

El Rey.

He heard it spoken with affection. With reverence. With quiet desperation. Once, he heard it used angrily, like an accusation, as if he'd failed to live up to something someone had decided he was supposed to be.

That one stayed with him longer than the others.

He learned to carry the name the way you carried something fragile. Carefully. Without letting it define the shape of your hands.

He wasn't a leader.

Leaders gathered people and pointed them somewhere.

Rey did neither.

He didn't organize. He didn't rally. He didn't speak in front of crowds unless he had a guitar in his hands, and even then he spoke only through sound. He didn't tell people what to feel. He didn't tell them what to believe.

He gave them space.

That was it.

Space to grieve without being corrected. Space to remember without being rushed. Space to sit in silence together without someone telling them it was time to move on.

The city didn't know what to do with that.

Systems were built to absorb threats, not witnesses.

Once, a man from a local station tracked him down after a show and asked if he wanted to "expand his reach." Rey listened politely, nodded at the right places, and declined without giving a reason.

Another time, someone offered to set up recurring performances at sanctioned venues. Better sound. Better pay. Better exposure.

Rey shook his head.

He didn't explain that exposure was just another word for surveillance. That stages came with expectations. That once the city decided you were useful, it started deciding what you were for.

He played in places where there were no contracts and no cameras. Where the sound system was held together with duct tape and patience. Where people didn't clap because they were supposed to, but because something inside them demanded release.

He learned which neighborhoods needed him most.

Not the ones closest to the lights.

The ones where people still whispered about the day the doors closed like it had happened last week. The ones where kids grew up never knowing a world without the Wall and still somehow carried grief for something they'd never seen.

Once, after a show in a place that barely qualified as a bar, a young boy approached him holding a battered acoustic guitar with strings that didn't match.

"My mom says you make sad songs," the boy said.

Rey smiled faintly. "I do."

The boy frowned, considering this. "Can you show me how?"

Rey took the guitar gently, tuned it as best he could, and showed the boy a simple chord progression. Nothing fancy. Just something that worked.

The boy played it once, fingers clumsy and earnest.

The sound was wrong.

Rey nodded. "Good start."

The boy grinned like he'd just been handed a secret.

That was how it spread.

Not through fame.

Through imitation.

Rey never visited the Wall.

Not up close.

He didn't need to. It lived in him already. In his posture. In the way he flinched at sudden metal sounds. In the way he never stood with his back to a crowd.

But sometimes, late at night, he played close enough that the sound carried.

Not toward the city.

Toward the concrete.

He didn't know if it mattered. Didn't know if anyone on the other side could hear it. Didn't know if the Wall remembered the people it crushed or if it was just another structure doing what it had been designed to do.

He played anyway.

Because sound had a way of seeping into places steel couldn't seal.

Rey never spoke Amara's name on stage.

He didn't need to.

She lived in every pause between chords. In the way he waited a second longer than necessary before starting. In the way he always packed up carefully, like someone might need the instrument again.

Some nights, after shows, he walked the city until his legs ached. Past murals layered over older murals. Past checkpoints that barely glanced at him anymore. Past people who nodded and looked away like they didn't want to intrude on whatever he was carrying.

He walked until the city quieted enough that he could hear his own breathing.

On one of those nights, he passed a group sitting on a curb, sharing a cheap speaker and laughing too loudly. One of them recognized him and started to say his name.

Rey lifted a finger to his lips.

Not in warning.

In gratitude.

They nodded and let him pass.

By the time dawn came, the city looked almost peaceful. The neon dimmed. The drones shifted patterns. The Wall stood exactly where it always had, massive and indifferent.

Rey sat on the edge of a rooftop somewhere no one important cared about and watched the light change.

He thought about Lidia and Mateo, wherever they were. Thought about the life they might've lived. Thought about how many people carried versions of that same thought every morning without ever speaking it.

He thought about how the city would keep moving no matter what he did.

And he thought about how sometimes, moving wasn't the point.

Rey picked up his guitar and played quietly to the waking city.

Not a song about loss.

Not a song about the Wall.

Just a song.

For the people who stayed.

For the people who remembered.

For the people who needed to hear something honest before the noise returned.

They would never build statues for him.

They would never put his name on anything official.

And that was fine.

Because The Rey wasn't meant to be remembered.

He was meant to be *felt*.

And somewhere, in a bar that hadn't existed yesterday and wouldn't exist tomorrow, someone would hear a song and realize they weren't alone.

That was enough.

That had always been enough.

END

This account stands alone.

It is also a prelude.

The events that shaped Rey's world are explored further in *Echoes of War*—the first mainline novel in **The Eradication Archive**, where the consequences of Eradication unfold on a much larger scale.

Some voices whisper.

Others become war.